NEW HAVEN PUBLIC LIBRARY

3 5000 09471 21

W9-DIY-185

OFFICIALLY W

RY

Condition Noted 08-25-2016

FAIR HAVEN LIBRARY
182 GRAND AVENUE
NEW HAVEN CT 06513

# A Note to Parents

OFFICIAL NEW HAVEN FREE PUBLIC LIBRARY

DK READERS is a compelling program for beginning readers, designed in conjunction with leading literacy experts, including Dr. Linda Gambrell, Professor of Education at Clemson University. Dr. Gambrell has served as President of the National Reading Conference and the College Reading Association, and has recently been elected to serve as President of the International Reading Association.

Beautiful illustrations and superb full-color photographs combine with engaging, easy-to-read stories and informational texts to offer a fresh approach to each subject in the series. Each DK READER is guaranteed to capture a child's interest while developing his or her reading skills, general knowledge, and love of reading.

The five levels of DK READERS are aimed at different reading abilities, enabling you to choose the books that are exactly right for your child:

**Pre-level 1**: Learning to read

**Level 1**: Beginning to read

**Level 2**: Beginning to read alone

**Level 3**: Reading alone

**Level 4**: Proficient readers

The "normal" age at which a child begins to read can be anywhere from three to eight years old. Adult participation through the lower levels is very helpful for providing encouragement, discussing storylines, and sounding out unfamiliar words.

No matter which level you select, you can be sure that you are helping your child learn to read, then read to learn!

LONDON, NEW YORK, MUNICH,
MELBOURNE, AND DELHI

**For Dorling Kindersley**
**Project Editor** Heather Scott
**Designer** Owen Bennett
**Brand Manager** Lisa Lanzarini
**Publishing Manager** Simon Beecroft
**Category Publisher** Alex Allan
**Production Controller** Nick Seston
**Production Editor** Sean Daly

**For Lucasfilm**
**Executive Editor** Jonathan W. Rinzler
**Art Director** Troy Alders
**Keeper of the Holocron** Leland Chee
**Director of Publishing** Carol Roeder

**Reading Consultant**
Linda B. Gambrell, Ph.D.

This book is dedicated to Linus Beecroft

First published in the United States in 2008 by
DK Publishing
375 Hudson Street,
New York, New York 10014

08 09 10 11 10 9 8 7 6 5 4 3

SD345—05/08

Copyright © 2008 Lucasfilm Ltd. and ™
Page design copyright © 2008 Dorling Kindersley Limited

All rights reserved under International and Pan-American Copyright
Conventions. No part of this publication may be reproduced, stored in a
retrieval system, or transmitted in any form or by any means, electronic,
mechanical, photocopying, recording, or otherwise, without the prior
written permission of the copyright owner.

DK Books are available at special discounts when purchased in bulk for
sales promotions, premiums, fund-raising, or educational use.
For details, contact: DK Publishing Special Markets,
375 Hudson Street, New York, New York 10014
SpecialSales@dk.com

Published in Great Britain by Dorling Kindersley Limited.
A catalog record for this book is available from the Library of Congress.

ISBN: 978-0-7566-4031-6 (Paperback)
ISBN: 978-0-7566-4030-9 (Hardback)

Color reproduction by Alta Image, UK
Printed and bound in the U.S.A. by Lake Book Manufacturing, Inc.

Discover more at
**www.dk.com**
**www.starwars.com**

READER BEECROFT
Star Wars, the clone wa
35000094712147
FAIRHAVEN

**DK READERS**

# STAR WARS®

## THE CLONE WARS™

## Anakin In Action!

Written by Simon Beecroft

A group of gunships fly through
the sky.
Each gunship carries soldiers
and Jedi generals.
The gunships are flying very fast.
They are on a dangerous mission.

## Gunships
Gunships carry soldiers into battle.

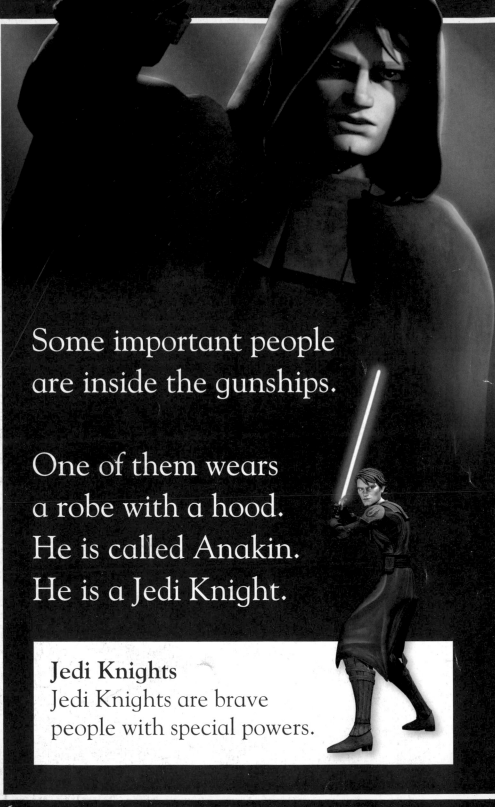

Some important people
are inside the gunships.

One of them wears
a robe with a hood.
He is called Anakin.
He is a Jedi Knight.

**Jedi Knights**
Jedi Knights are brave
people with special powers.

A soldier stands next to Anakin.
This soldier is Captain Rex.
Captain Rex wears a special
helmet over his face.
His body is protected by armor.

Another Jedi is traveling in
the gunship with Anakin.
Her name is Ahsoka.
Ahsoka is still learning her Jedi
powers. Anakin is her teacher.

Ahsoka has special
white patterns on her red skin.
She also has long head tails.

**Alien Jedi**
Ahsoka is an alien.
Aliens are different
from humans.
They come from
other worlds.

Anakin, Ahsoka, and the clone soldiers land close to a big castle.

They are going to rescue a young creature called Rotta.
Rotta is a prisoner inside the castle.

Anakin is ready
with his lightsaber!

**Clone soldiers**
Clones are
humans who all
look and behave
the same way.

Enemy droids stand at the top of the castle wall. They see Anakin and the others land.

Spider droids have red eyes and walk on four mechanical legs. They start firing their big guns.

Battle droids also start firing.
Watch out Anakin!

**Droid soldiers**
Battle droids are not
human soldiers. They
are machine soldiers.

Anakin, Ahsoka, and the clone
soldiers reach the castle wall.
It is so high they can hardly see
the top.
Captain Rex fires ropes out of his
blaster. The ropes hook onto the
top of the wall.

The Jedi and the soldiers all grab
hold of the ropes and start
climbing up. Anakin goes first and
Ahsoka follows close behind.
Clone soldiers in big tanks also
start climbing the wall.

**Clone tanks**
These big tanks
walk on six powerful
legs. They can also
climb walls.

Anakin has almost reached the top of the castle wall when battle droids on flying machines start to attack. Anakin thinks quickly.

He jumps onto one of the machines as it flies past.

**STAPs**
These flying machines are called STAPs. They have blaster cannons on the front.

Anakin kicks the droid off his
flying machine.
Now he attacks the other droids!

After a lot of fighting, Anakin and Ahsoka reach the top of the castle wall.
They enter the castle.
The castle is cold and dark.

**Baby Hutt**
Rotta is a creature called a Hutt. Ahsoka carries him in a backpack.

Anakin and Ahsoka sneak along the creepy corridors. Soon, they are able to find Rotta. He is just a baby. They must rescue Rotta quickly. They must leave the castle quickly.

Too late! The droids
have blocked the exit.
Someone is with them.
This person looks dangerous.
She holds a lightsaber with
a red blade.

Her name is Ventress.
She has special powers like a Jedi.
Anakin, Ahsoka, and Captain Rex
run back inside the castle
and lock the door.

Ventress breaks down the door to
the castle. She goes inside to look
for Anakin and Ahsoka.

In a dark room, Ventress finds
Anakin and Ahsoka.
Anakin has nowhere to run.
He lights his blue lightsaber.
Ventress and Anakin fight each
other with their lightsabers.
Clash!

**Jedi enemy**
Ventress uses a
lightsaber like a Jedi.
But she is not a Jedi.
She is a deadly
enemy of the Jedi.

Ahsoka is looking after Rotta.
She is carrying him on her back.
But she sees that Anakin needs
her help.

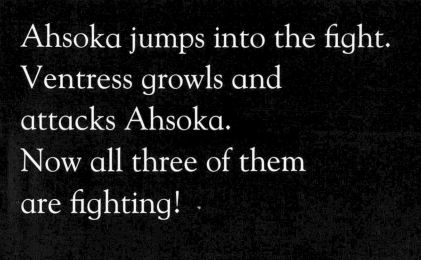

Ahsoka jumps into the fight.
Ventress growls and
attacks Ahsoka.
Now all three of them
are fighting! ·

Ahsoka tries to find a way out of the dark room. She opens a heavy door. Big mistake!

A huge monstrous shape comes out of the shadows.
It is a rancor monster.

The rancor has sharp teeth and claws. It roars and attacks!

**Rancors**
Rancors are dangerous monsters with big heads and sharp claws and teeth.

Anakin and Ventress jump
onto the rancor's back
and continue fighting.
The rancor is confused.
It can no longer see Anakin
and Ventress.

Then the rancor
spots Ahsoka
and Rotta.

It moves toward them, as Anakin
and Ventress fight on its back.
Ahsoka stabs the rancor's foot.

It howls in pain and falls right
on top of Ventress. Squish!

Anakin and Ahsoka
think that the
rancor has crushed
Ventress. They
escape from the
castle with Rotta.

But after they have
gone, there is a
noise: vzzz!

It is a lightsaber being turned on.
Ventress is still alive!

Outside, Anakin tells Ahsoka
she was a great Jedi today.
A gunship arrives to take
them away. They are off
on another adventure!

# Clone Wars Facts

Anakin Skywalker uses a lightsaber with a glowing blue blade.

Ahsoka uses a lightsaber with a green blade.

Ventress's lightsabers have red blades.

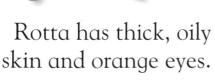

Captain Rex goes on missions with Anakin.

Rotta has thick, oily skin and orange eyes.

09 09